Nurse Clementine

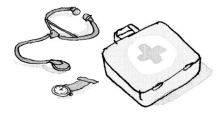

First U.S. edition 2013

Library of Congress Cataloging-in-Publication Data is available.

Library of Congress Catalog Card Number pending

ISBN 978-0-7636-6382-7

13 14 15 16 17 18 SCP 10 9 8 7 6 5 4 3 2 1

Printed in Humen, Dongguan, China

This book was typeset in Goudy.
The illustrations were done in watercolor and ink.

Candlewick Press
99 Dover Street
Somerville, Massachusetts 02144

visit us at www.candlewick.com

Simon James

Nurse Clementine

CANDLEWICK PRESS

It was Clementine Brown's birthday.
Mr. and Mrs. Brown bought her
a nurse's outfit and a first-aid kit.

"It's just what I wanted," she said.

"You can call me Nurse Clementine from now on!"

Nurse Clementine didn't have to wait long for her first emergency.

Mr. Brown banged his toe on the living-room door.

Nurse Clementine got right to work.

"You'll need to keep this on for a week," she said.

"A week?" moaned Mr. Brown.

"A week," said Nurse Clementine firmly.

Next, Mrs. Brown complained that she had a headache. Nurse Clementine gave her a complete checkup.

Her ears were okay, her tongue wasn't spotty, and her temperature was normal.

So, just to be safe, Nurse Clementine bandaged her head.

"You'll have to keep this on for a week," she said.

"A week?" Mrs. Brown said with a sigh.

"A week," said Nurse Clementine firmly.

In the kitchen,
Nurse Clementine
found Wellington,
licking his paw.

It must be sore, decided
Nurse Clementine.
She bandaged it up
as best she could.

Nurse Clementine was very pleased with her
work. She rushed off to find her brother, Tommy.
He was bound to need some help.

Bold and fearless, Tommy the superhero
was on his way down the stairs.

"Look out, Tommy!" shouted Clementine.

"You're going to hit—"

"The door!" Nurse Clementine immediately opened
her first-aid kit. "It's a good thing I'm here," she said.

"No, it's not!" said Tommy. "I don't need a nurse."

"I'm Super Tommy. Watch me fly!
I can leap from sofas."

"Look out, Tommy!"
said Clementine.
"You're going to hit—"

"The floor!"
"Ouch!" said Tommy.

Nurse Clementine rushed over with her stethoscope.
She told Tommy to keep still while she checked
him for breaks and bruises.

"I'm not broken," said Tommy. "And I told you before, I *don't* need a nurse. Leave me alone!"

Tommy marched off toward the backyard.

Clementine sat while Tommy played.

There was no one left to take care of.

She would just have to practice nursing by herself.
First she listened to her own heartbeat.

Then she practiced
bandaging the
drainpipe.

But it was no good.
"Nurses need someone to take
care of," Clementine said
with a sigh.

Then she heard a voice calling
from up in the tree.
"Clementine! Clementine!
Help!" It was Tommy.

"I'm stuck!" he cried. "I can't get down.
   It's too high!"

"Hang on, Tommy!"
called Clementine.
"I'll get you down."

Clementine knew
she had to think
quickly.

After all, this was
a **real** emergency.

Clementine stood on tiptoe, but she couldn't reach Tommy.

"I'm slipping," he said.

"Hold on," said Nurse Clementine.

"I can't!" said Tommy. "I'm going to fall!"

Tommy closed his eyes as his hands slipped.

But Nurse Clementine was there to catch him.

"I've got you," she said.

Tommy was relieved to be back on the ground.
"Thanks, Clementine," he said. "You were great!"

When Tommy turned
to go, Clementine
noticed something.
"Tommy," she said,
"you scraped your arm!"
"Did I?" said Tommy.

"You can bandage it
if you like."

Nurse Clementine
was delighted to help.
This was going to
be her best bandage
yet. But there was one
small problem. . . .

She had forgotten her scissors!

"This is going to be an extra-
special superhero bandage,"
said Nurse Clementine.
"Really?" said Tommy.
"But you're going to
have to keep it on
all week," said
Clementine firmly.

"All week?" said Tommy. "Great!"

The End

Stethoscope

Watch

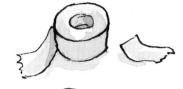

Tape

Eye Patch

Chocolate

Blood-Pressure Monitor

Case

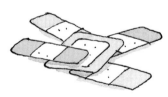

Band-Aids

Bandage

Otoscope

Name Badge

Reflex Hammer

Tongue Depressor

More Bandages

Cap

Thermometer

Gloves

Cotton Balls

Pen light

Scissors

Emergency Toffees

First-Aid Book

Tweezers

Wipes